D1541059

The Saturday Night Stalker

A STORY ABOUT NIGHTMARES

Written by
JOY BERRY

WORD INC.
Waco, Texas 76796

About the Author and Publisher

Joy Berry's mission in life is to help families cope with everyday problems and to help children become competent, responsible, happy individuals. To achieve her goal, she has written over two hundred self-help books for children from infancy through age twelve. Her work has revolutionized children's publishing by providing families with practical, how-to, living skills information that was previously unavailable in children's books.

Joy has gathered a dedicated team of experts, including psychologists, educators, child developmentalists, writers, editors, designers, and artists to form her publishing company and to help produce her work.

The company, Living Skills Press, produces thoroughly researched books and audiovisual materials that successfully combine humor and education to teach children subjects ranging from how to clean a bedroom to how to resolve problems and get along with other people.

Managing Editor: Ellen Klarberg
Copy Editor: Kate Dickey
Contributing Editors: Chris Clarke, Susan Motycka
Editorial Assistant: Lana Eberhard

Art Director: Laurie Westdahl
Assistant Art Director: Caroline Rennard
Designer: Laurie Westdahl
Production: Margaret Parks
Illustration Design: Bartholomew
Inker: Berenice Happé Iriks
Colorer: Berenice Happé Iriks
Composition: TBH/Typecast, Inc.
Published by Word Incorporated
in cooperation with Living Skills Press

Hello, my name is Joy, and I'd like to tell you a story about Casey and a valuable lesson he learned about nightmares.

"Let's tell ghost stories," A.J. suggested when boredom set in at the Human Race Club overnighter.

"That's a great idea!" Casey said excitedly.

"I've got one," Teddy offered. And when no one seemed to object to his being the first to tell a story, he began speaking in a sinister tone. "Once there was this guy who fell in a swamp . . ."

"You told that one at our last camp out," Maggie said blandly.

Teddy thought about Maggie's remark. "Hmmm, maybe you're right," he said. Then in an effort to retain the attention of his audience, he quickly resumed his storytelling mode and began again. "Once there were five fraternity brothers who decided to have a 20-year reunion . . ."

Maggie sighed out loud. "You also told us that one," she said impatiently.

Undaunted by Maggie's insensitive interruptions, Teddy proposed a third story. "Have I ever told you guys the one about the haunted beach house?"

"Yep," Maggie said coldly.

Teddy scanned the faces of the other club members. And when no one attempted to refute Maggie's objections, he decided to put his critic on the spot.

"Well, Maggie," Teddy said pointedly, "since you've already heard all of *my* stories, maybe *you'd* like to tell one!"

Maggie looked away quickly and began to fidget.

"No way!" A.J. protested. "I'm not listening to any of Maggie's stupid stories!"

"*You're* criticizing *my* stories?" Maggie yelled. "At least *I* can remember the endings to *my* stories. *You* never remember the endings to *yours*!"

"Maybe we should pop some popcorn," Casey recommended sheepishly.

"Not now!" Maggie and A.J. said in unison. A hush fell over the entire group.

Finally, after what seemed to be an awfully long time, Pamela's small voice broke the silence. "I know an interesting story that you might not have heard."

Four surprised club members turned their eyes toward Pamela. She had never told the group a ghost story before and everyone had automatically assumed that she didn't like doing that kind of thing.

"*You* know a ghost story?" a disbelieving A.J. asked.

"Not exactly," Pamela answered, trying to be as accurate as possible. "It isn't a ghost story but it *is* scary. It's been in all the newspapers lately."

By this time Pamela had captured everyone's interest, and the spellbound look on each club member's face implored her to tell her story.

"There's this man they call the Saturday Night Stalker," Pamela said ominously. "He has committed at least six brutal murders in approximately six months. All of the people he has killed are under the age of thirteen."

No one dared to move a muscle for fear that Pamela would be distracted and stop talking.

"According to the police reports," she continued, "the murderer stalks his victims for several days before he kills them."

Teddy, A.J., and Maggie swallowed hard, and a naive Casey asked, "Is that why they call him a stalker?"

"Of course it is, you dummy!" A.J. grumbled at Casey. Then he turned back to Pamela. "But why do they call him the *Saturday* Night Stalker?"

"Because he always kills his victims on a Saturday night," Pamela said somberly.

Now it was Teddy's turn to pose a question and he asked the one that was on everyone's mind. "How does he do it?" he inquired.

Pamela hesitated as though the answer to Teddy's question were too horrible to put into words. "How do you think he does it?" she asked the group.

Four wide-eyed kids shook their heads as they continued to stare at Pamela.

"Oh, Pamela, just tell us!" Maggie demanded.
Pamela faltered. "He . . . he smothers them to death."

The news about the Saturday Night Stalker led to an intense exchange among the club members, each one sharing gruesome accounts of real-life murders. And, just as A.J. had hoped, the gory conversation helped liven up the club get-together. At first A.J.'s idea about telling ghost stories seemed appropriate for the occasion, but that was only because it was still light outside. As night came, the excitement of telling and listening to scary stories gave way to an almost uncontrollable fear.

Needless to say, the club members got very little sleep during the night. And when they returned to their homes the next day, they were exhausted.

Casey was affected deeply by the frightening murder stories, especially the one Pamela had told. For as long as he could remember, Casey had hated having anything cover his face. So he could not imagine anything worse than being smothered to death.

On the night after the club get-together, an unfamiliar noise aroused Casey from a deep sleep. As he opened his eyes he saw a shadowy figure pass by his bedroom window. Convinced that what he had seen was the Saturday Night Stalker, Casey bounded out of bed and ran to his parents' bedroom.

"He's going to smother me to death!" he screamed.

Casey's hysterical cry awakened his mother and father suddenly. "What are you talking about?" Mr. O'Reilly asked while rubbing the sleep from his eyes.

"I saw him!" Casey said breathlessly. "He was right outside my window!"

Mrs. O'Reilly took hold of her son's hand and tried to calm him down. "*Who* was outside your window?" she asked protectively.

Frustrated because his parents did not seem to comprehend the magnitude of his problem, Casey shouted, "The Saturday Night Stalker!"

Both parents heaved sighs of relief. Then Mr. O'Reilly explained to Casey that the Saturday Night Stalker had recently been captured.

"But what if he's escaped?" Casey asked anxiously.

When nothing either parent could say seemed to console their son, Mr. O'Reilly offered to check the area outside Casey's bedroom. Armed with a flashlight, he disappeared into the night while Casey snuggled close to his mother in his parents' bed.

A few moments later Mr. O'Reilly reappeared. "All clear!" he announced.

In spite of his father's reassurance, Casey was still visibly fearful.

"You can sleep in our bed if you want to, Casey," Mrs. O'Reilly said dotingly.

Casey nestled into a comfortable position. "I want to," he said. And with that he fell asleep.

For the remainder of that night and for several nights afterwards, Casey's sleep was plagued by recurring bad dreams about the Saturday Night Stalker. These dreams would have most likely subsided, had it not been for the fact that Casey continued to see the shadowy figure pass by his window at about the same time every night.

With each day Casey became more certain that the Saturday Night Stalker was stalking *him*! At first Mr. and Mrs. O'Reilly were concerned about their son's safety. But when Mr. O'Reilly's flashlight searches failed to turn up any evidence of the person Casey was supposed to have seen, Mr. and Mrs. O'Reilly started to worry about their son's vivid imagination.

"But it's not all in my mind! I really *have* seen someone outside my window!" Casey argued plaintively.

Casey's father finally decided to sleep in Casey's room so he could see the supposed killer for himself.

At approximately 10 o'clock on Saturday night Casey awoke, sat straight up in bed, and shrieked, "It's him! It's him!"

His son's screams jolted Mr. O'Reilly out of his sleep just in time to see the shadowy form that was frightening his son. He jumped out of bed, rushed to the window, and threw it open. "Hey you!" he called out. "What are you doing?"

Casey was frozen in his bed. With both his hands covering his face, he peeked between his fingers to see who his father was talking to.

Before long Mr. O'Reilly turned and addressed his son. "Casey, I want you to meet your Saturday Night Stalker."

Casey's father stepped aside from the window to reveal a familiar figure dressed in a sweatsuit. It was the O'Reillys' next-door neighbor.

"Mr. Abrams, it's you!" Casey gasped. "What are you doing out there?"

"I'm going jogging! I've found that late evening is the very best time for me to run!" Mr. Abrams replied. Casey sank back onto his pillow in relief.

The two men chatted for a while and then said goodnight. Mr. O'Reilly closed the window and returned to Casey's bedside.

"Casey, I hope you realize the stories you and your friends exchanged at the overnighter contributed to your having a pretty rough week."

Mr. O'Reilly talked on and on. But before he could finish, Casey had fallen asleep.

The next day Casey attended a club meeting. "Let's tell scary stories!" Pamela suggested. "It was so much fun the last time we did it!"

Casey's heart raced. He knew he could not handle any more scary stories, but he was too embarrassed to admit it. He was afraid his friends might think he was a baby.

Just then A.J. spoke up. "Count me out, Pamela. The last time we told scary stories I had nightmares for a week!"

"Me too!" Maggie agreed.

"My nightmares were so bad, I had to sleep with my parents a couple of times," Teddy admitted.

"Me too," Maggie agreed again.

There was a long pause and then Casey suggested, "We could always pop some popcorn!"

"Now that's what I call a great idea!" Teddy said enthusiastically. And everyone, including Pamela, cheered.

So, what can we learn from all of this?

Casey was embarrassed about having nightmares. However, as he discovered at the club meeting, he didn't need to be embarrassed because he was not the only person who had nightmares.

Everyone has nightmares and everyone reacts to them. Remembering this the next time you have a nightmare will make you feel better.

There are several things Casey could have done to comfort himself when he had a nightmare.

He could have turned on his light and looked around the room to make sure everything was OK. He also could have concentrated on pleasant memories, expectations, or hopes. This would have allowed him to replace his scary thoughts with positive thoughts.

Turning on your light, checking your room, and thinking positive thoughts can make you feel better the next time you have a nightmare.

Casey did the right thing when he had recurring nightmares that interfered with his sleep. He asked for help and then accepted it when it was given to him.

It is important that you get help right away whenever you feel overwhelmed by frightening thoughts or dreams.

Casey learned the hard way that scary thoughts can turn into frightening nightmares. Scary thoughts can come from

- watching scary movies,
- listening to scary stories, and
- thinking unpleasant thoughts at bedtime.

You will most likely have fewer nightmares if you avoid doing these activities.

EPILOGUE

Not long ago I was talking with the club members about nightmares. Our discussion prompted Casey to tell us about *his* Saturday Night Stalker. Of course Casey's story gave everyone a good laugh. But when all was said and done, no one laughed louder than Casey.